MONIQUE

A Novella by Luísa Coelho

Translated from the Portuguese by
Dolores DeLuise & Maria do Carmo de Vasconcelos

Monique

By Luísa Coelho
Translated from the Portuguese by Dolores DeLuise
and Maria do Carmo de Vasconcelos

Copyright 2007

ISBN: 978-1-929355-26-6

Library of Congress Control Number: 2005910528

Second Printing: ISBN 978-1-7370520-7-4

Design and composition by Susan Ramundo and Karen Kang
Cover by Isabel Pavão
Photos of translators by Zhanna Yablokova

Published by Pleasure Boat Studio: A Literary Press
201 West 89 Street
New York, NY 10024
Tel/Fax: 888-810-5308
e-mail: *pleasboat@nyc.rr.com*
URL: *www.pleasureboatstudio.com*

Dedication

In Memory of
Rashelle Trefousse

Acknowledgments

We would like to thank Carl Pellman, all our friends and family; we would particularly like to thank Ariel Pellman for her assistance.

In addition, we are grateful to our colleagues and staff at Borough of Manhattan Community College of the City University of New York, particularly Jane Young and Phil Eggers.

Thanks to author Luísa Coelho; cover artist Isabel Pavão; photographer Zhanna Yablokova; designers Karen Kang and Susan Ramundo; and our publisher, Jack Estes.

Thanks as well to Catulina Guerreiro, who introduced us to the book, and special thanks to Sara Bershtel.

Translators' Note

There exist some excellent translations of Portuguese fiction, most outstandingly by the prolific Gregory Rabassa (who has translated such notable authors as João de Melo, Mário de Carvalho, António Lobo Atunes, Joachim Machado de Assis and Jorge Amado). Rabassa has greatly promoted an interest in Portuguese-language fiction although he himself is not a native speaker. What we hope to contribute to the future of Portuguese literature in the United States is an emphasis on the constituent cultural and linguistic proficiency of two native speakers—Portuguese and English—hitherto unapplied to Portuguese translations. Our work is characterized by a precise rendering of cultural, literary, and linguistic nuances in both Portuguese and English.

This translation is the result of a process of negotiation between two different languages and their idioms and two different cultural memories. First and foremost, we have attempted to honor the fact that language creates culture, as, of course, culture creates language. To fulfill our hope that our translation would welcome English-speaking readers into a Portuguese text, we had to make some choices; for example, for graphical reasons we adjusted some boundaries by substituting semi-colons for commas and dividing paragraphs that encompassed many topics; likewise, for stylistic reasons we connected simple sentences. Additionally, the indeterminate subject, so evocative in Portuguese, was made explicit in English, when possible, through inclusion of subject nouns and pronouns. Further, we literalized certain metaphors and at other times replaced metaphors with their English equivalents, to represent, as closely as possible, the exchange of cultural sensibilities.

Our technique of negotiation in translation makes use of our collective knowledge of languages, literature, and other fields such as film theory, theater, philology, art history, women's studies, gender studies, as well as studio painting and sculpture. We have lectured on this technique and have published and lectured on the method of pedagogy developed as a result of having worked on this particular novella.

—*Dolores DeLuise & Maria do Carmo de Vasconcelos*

Introduction

In 1929, Marguerite Yourcenar, writing in French, published her first novel, *Alexis, or a Treatise on a Vain Conflict*,[1] in the form of a letter written by a husband to the wife of three years whom he had deserted.

During their marriage, Alexis perceived his wife as a beautiful, kind, ethical, attentive woman, yet he was nevertheless unable to fulfill his obligations to her. He was so focused on his own needs that he was totally uninterested in hers. He was completely incapable of imagining a woman's sexual needs; indeed, a "woman's sexual needs" was scarcely a category in the 1920s. We learn that the matrix of his existence is his music, somehow intermingled with the fact of his homosexuality, also not a category of discourse in the '20s.[2] When he decides to pursue music, we are given to understand it is homosexuality he pursues as well.

Alexis receives no response to his letter for more than seventy years, and although Yourcenar had never been able to do it herself, she had hoped someone would answer him. In 2003, the Portuguese author, Luísa Coelho took up the task and created *Monique* in response to Yourcenar's *Alexis*. Coelho's novella, the letter Monique wrote in return to Alexis, explodes not only Alexis's perception of Monique, but society's perception of women as well. In it, she opens the door to an inner life

---

[1] Or, more idiomatically translated, *Alexis, or a Losing Battle.*
[2] With exceptions, however, most notably André Gide.

unimaginable by both her husband and the society in which she lived. She was born in and becomes associated with an exotic Caribbean landscape, which is later seen in dramatic juxtaposition to the dreary landscape of the north of France that is linked with a repressive Christianity.

Monique has a lonely childhood, enlivened only by her father's infrequent visits home. While she remembers her mother only as an invalid, she recalls her father's life of activity—a botanical adventurer on a perpetual quest for exotic plants. He teaches her Latin, which she, in turn, teaches her parakeet companions to whom she had turned in her loneliness, as Coelho invokes the tradition of magical realism of the New World. On his visits home, she tells us, she and her father "construct" the world together, and she identifies herself strongly with him. To be sure, her education is solidly gendered; she studies the language of the Fathers with her own father, and becomes schooled in the traditional medieval curriculum in a language other than the vernacular, absorbing, along with that language, the received hierarchies of Western institutions. Ironically, however, she makes the language of public education her own private idiom within which she is able to discover freedom from the laws of civilization. She appropriates the tradition of authority passed down from one Latinate discourse to another, and the hierarchy shatters, the notion of authority becomes transformed, and she thereby establishes herself as her own authority. When her parakeets speak the Latin she had taught them, they are, in a sense, citing her as their authority. In the religious context of the story we become able to see the parakeets parodying worshipers in church, mouthing prayers, not in their own vernacular, but in a Latin they don't understand. Completing this trope in a small flourish toward the end of the story, we hear that

Monique's grown son had visited the island to which she had never returned, and reported that generations of parakeets had been known to speak Latin and were speaking it still.

Her mother's absence, her identification with her father, their idealized relationship, and her interest in the male sphere serve to make her uniquely independent and resourceful and uninterested in the realm of feminine domesticity. Upon her mother's death, she is taken to live with her father's parents in the north of France. Her existence in her Caribbean dream world is abruptly terminated, but the memory of it sustains her creativity and her very life for the rest of her days. Her paternal grandparents soon send her to a religious boarding school run by nuns, and Monique becomes initiated into a world of sexuality inextricably linked to a Christian mysticism with sado-masochistic overtones.

Monique allows a re-reading of Alexis that makes clear his lack of knowledge of the woman to whom he had been married for three years. He knew nothing of her immense creativity and lesbian sexuality that had taught her to long for a passionate sexual relationship. Much worse, however, was the tragedy of Alexis's emotional isolation that prevented his interest in her inner life. He too was a victim of social circumstances that dictated he marry against his sexual preference. Despite all this, Monique continued to love him for the rest of her life.

After a long silence, Monique reveals that all is not the way it seemed to both Alexis, her former husband, and the readers of *Alexis*. Coelho grasps the problematics of gender, class, and society of a former time and demonstrates incredible insight into the politics of repression; she exposes, as well, the lack of early twentieth-century society's understanding of women's lives. Most astonishing is how *Monique* concludes and at the same time ruptures the circle begun by *Alexis*. Coelho animates the feminine spirit haunting *Alexis* by drawing out and giving voice to the woman placed there by Yourcenar but silenced by society.

—*Dolores DeLuise & Maria do Carmo de Vasconcelos*

Alexis,

It was only in the autumn of my pain that I received your letter, old friend. For three years, if my memory is correct, your words fluttered around like airborne seeds before coming to rest their burden on my eyes. We spent three years together, making our way through a precious, sacred forest, Alexis, filled with fountains and mysteries. I thought it would go on forever since I was never able to visualize it completely. In our last days as a couple, I remember experiencing it differently—freer and more secret still, if that were really possible.

Your music created a restlessness that pervaded our home, but strangely enough, it was soothing to our little Daniel. His blue eyes, already open to the world, used to drift toward the musical notes that filled the air. At that time, your music was so invasive that it prevented the very act of listening. Today when I'm tormented by my difficulty hearing, I'm finally able to listen to my memories and allow them to speak.

I thought about it a long time before I began writing this letter—fifty years, to be exact. The right time is now; it will never come again. Later on, I'll talk about the pain you caused when you left. Later on, I'll talk about the pain you caused when you ignored your obligations. But right now I'm going to tell you about my early life, when all time was future time, when all time was harvest time. You don't know a thing about that part of my life because we never got to talk about it. Our own childhood is something we cannot share with others; we can only take someone on a tour through it, and discovering me was never something you wanted to do. But I want to tell you about my birthplace in the French Antilles and how I left there. Although the path I traveled through childhood, Alexis, was filled with absences, there were some presences I cherished too.

1

MONIQUE

It was in a colonial house, not far from the city of Sainte-Pierre, on the island of Martinique that the Thiebaud family lived. My family. My father, my mother, and I: a sacred triangle. My dreams were centered at the bottom of the garden in a hut hidden by thick vegetation. My father used to leave for long periods of time, and that was when the entrance to that palace made of wood and shadow, where his riches rested, was inaccessible to me. Then with my open palms glued to the window pane, I pretended to touch the shadows lying on the table and cast onto the floor; shadows of my father's former presence. My father's far-away botanical discoveries lay there like maps. A cartography of memory. Fragments of life that had the power to explain the world. They opened up the start of my beginning.

My father had devoted his life to those discoveries. I lived only to watch as he conjured up his perfumes and scents, extracting floral spirituality. He was able to reconstruct the world. When he was at home, he worked in the hut; I sat on his lap where I too constructed the world, and together we fitted the pieces into the puzzle. And when I thought everything was ready and we could finally play, my father left again. He always wanted to know more, to investigate more thoroughly and farther and farther away. But I still remained expectant. I strolled through the park that surrounded the house. I leafed through the papers where he had been drawing. I looked at the lines that described a memory here and sketched out a meaning there. I studied his books, the research of Père Labat[1] on *The Natural History of the Antilles* or the four

---

[1] Jean-Baptiste Labat (1663–1738), French clergyman, botanist, writer, explorer, ethnographer, soldier, engineer, and landowner, served two years of missionary service on Martinique.

2

volumes of *Flora Antillarum* illustrated with the beautifully colored drawings of F. Richard de Tussac.[2] My hands smelled good; they smelled musty like the books in his library that had been touched by time. I was able to live inside of History. I spelled the Latin words that gave sense to the images. The sonorous implication of *solandra grandiflora*, the obscurity of the term *oncidium*, or, still more terrible, the word *trignocephalus*, all left me fascinated.

Latin was my first foreign language, and to this day I sometimes hear myself saying, "*ex nihilo nihil*," during the luminous snowy mornings of winter while I look out at the mountain that protects my house. As my father used to say when he marveled at the beauties of nature that he brought home: "Do you see my darling, everything that exists now in any way has always existed? All we do is create meaning for the fragments that we find." Nevertheless, today I speak Latin only to myself because, as with other precious things, this language lost itself along the way to progress, through superficiality and through the easy way out. It became useless. It's alive only on the pages of my father's books and in my unconscious.

In fact, only Latin has the power to decipher my feelings and express meanings that emanate from between the words themselves. In his *Dictionary of Received Ideas*,[3] Flaubert entered under "Latin": "Don't trust Latin citations: They always hide something inconvenient." It was exactly that concept that had lured me to Latin. I was captivated by the idea of hiding because, besides hiding something inconvenient, it also revealed a kind of freedom that could never be confined. It was through hiding that

---

[2]François Richard de Tussac (1744–1848), French illustrator, *Flores des Antilles* (1808-1827).

[3]1911, a satirical work that ridiculed social habits and language of the French.

Latin could say the unsayable. Its loss de-eroticized our language, and cost us a great deal of cultural memory.

During the first days after my father's return, I used to listen as he related his adventures, and then they became my adventures too. I knew how to recite the geographic contours of the Caribbean Sea and blow like the trade winds that smoothed and charmed his tales. My father arrived with the first rains, and that's why I always loved the rain, Alexis. It reminds me of my childhood. It returns me to a space of meditation, of intimacy and warmth. Of self-reflection. We're forced to listen to the rain as it makes us keep ourselves company. That's why most people don't like rain because it forces them to make contact with the center of their lives, occupy their own inner space, and speak to themselves. The rain doesn't listen to them; it makes itself heard, and, while they listen to it, they submerge themselves in the waters of memory. I, on the other hand, always liked those humid days of gray sky when the essence of the world's mystery is able to escape and awaken the damp black land. After the rain I like to talk about the game of listening. To discuss it. It's like after you make love: By listening to someone else's body, you learn about your own.

According to my childhood memories, my mother was always sick. I associate her image with the perfume of the periwinkle, the violet of death, *vinca minor*, with its leaves, shiny green, and its flowers, that very specific blue. They sent it to us from France, and we used it to staunch her hemorrhages: My mother was a sea of invisible blood; she was gradually being emptied of it. But what really puzzled me was the mystery of its loss because I never saw that red sea disappear. I thought the blood must have flowed out slowly through the edges of her curly hair like waves and washed up onto the sheets that were constantly being changed. Each day my mother became more transparent and fragile. Like glass. So I also thought she could be the victim of a vampire, a being from another world that I couldn't see, but whose presence I perceived in my mother's transparency. She was wasting away, each moment more feeble. The vampire frightened me because I sensed its presence without being able to construct an image of it, and what scared me still more was that I welcomed the pleasure that accompanied the fright. I entered my mother's room during the day to surprise the vampire, without really wanting to find it. During the night I would never have had the audacity to do that. What was going on, I think, was that to understand what was wrong with my mother, I needed to construct a fiction around it to better accept it.

My mother never left her room; the doctor had forbidden it. Sitting in an armchair, she used to look out through the large picture windows at the leaves dancing on the tree trunks in the garden, listen to the barking dog playing with the shadows of some inaccessible birds, and drink absinthe to suffocate her pain. She dreamed during the entire day, but at night I was never able to take her by surprise in her sleep. I was almost sure that my mother was a manatee, one of those creatures they call "mermaids," or "cowfish," who could only be captured by hunters who surprised them while they slept. Like a manatee, my mother was afraid to be surprised by death during her sleep. My mother had decided that would never happen; in fact, she died in a lucid moment. When my father was home, he was the one who cradled her, and if he weren't, it was anyone else who could provide her a warm body. It didn't matter who did it. Her nightgown was always white and faded, like her lips; the lace of her collar traced labyrinths on her skin. It was all white on white. I couldn't take my eyes off those colorless drawings; they choked me.

I never went near her. She frightened me and at the same time I felt sorry for myself because she was lost to me. Her brilliant gray expression was gone. She could hardly see.

Sometimes she tried to touch me. Her hands would approach my face, groping the air, trying to imprison me, and I would pull back, cringing against the door, forcing it, trying to escape. I felt her clammy, feverish hands in my nightmares until Daniel was born. After that, they disappeared, but now it's only the grayness of her look that still haunts me. Especially when I look at myself in the mirror. Her look is reflected back to me. Cloudy. But I never could see very well anyway.

When I was born, my father wasn't home. Or even on the island. He was exploring the world as usual. Both Dr. Adalberto (who later brought the sour and absinthe-dreaming calmness to my mother) and the midwife (who, in agreement with the ritual, asked that my placenta be buried under a tree in our garden, specifically a rose laurel, *podocarpus*) came to lend me a little courage. My difficulty wasn't finding the strength to enter this world we live in, but gathering the courage to abandon the primordial home forever. There is no return from birth, Alexis. It is our first suffering. The maternal shell is paradise. The lost paradise. And besides that, in Martinique, as in some European countries, a child born with a full head of hair is a child blessed with luck. But when I was born, my head was impoverished of hair. I was born, you could say, with less possibility. My mother, who had left France with my father several years before, had expected me impatiently, but when I finally arrived, she wasn't really there anymore. Her absence created my first emptiness. She existed, my mother, but she had no warmth; I felt cold in her presence.

I really don't know what words to use to tell you about my mother. She wasn't pretty, but I think if she had survived, she would have been what is referred to as a "very beautiful older woman" because she was like her own mother. I know, old friend, that my maternal grandmother frightened you a bit by the way she used her hands to communicate. Her hands could do her talking for her all by themselves. You spoke sometimes about what you called her "hypnotic power," thinking you understood her much better than others. Today I understand you. As a pianist, your hands are your voice. Maybe that was the reason I couldn't hear you. You never touched me very much, Alexis.

It is possible that I've confused my mother and my maternal grandmother in my memories. I imagine them as one, but in different settings. My mother is the heat and perspiration of the tropics, my grandmother, the cold and goosebumps of the north of France. My grandmother's name was Anna-Cornelia. My mother's name was a little sweeter and more perfumed, and it had certainly attracted my father: the name of a flower, Marguerite. They both had the same hands. Perhaps you can understand now, my sweet love, if I tell you that these two women in my life didn't contribute much to my formation, except maybe to develop in me the desire of being closer to men, of wanting to be a boy, and having the right to explore the *Montanha Pelada* of my childhood.[4]

When I was a child, living near the city of Sainte-Pierre, I was very happy and somewhat savage for the customs of the time. My mother's illness and my father's absence gave me freedom unknown to young girls of my age and social status. I could go barefoot in the park, sit on the ground, and take a shower under tropical rains whose force annihilated everything

---

[4]In 1902, Montanha Pelada (Bald Mountain, or, metaphorically the naked mountain) erupted and the city of Sainte-Pierre in Martinique was destroyed.

and whose noise suffocated my mother's cries. I owned domesticated birds: green parakeets, with whom I spoke Latin and a trained pelican who was a great fisherman. My favorite parakeet was named Prima Luce and the pelican answered to Thesaurus. Next to my father, they were my closest confidantes. I used to go to bed early, completely exhausted, and the next day, I awakened the sun who in turn awakened Prima Luce. It was his responsibility to pronounce the first words of the day; the dawn always discovered him talking.

The people around me, the servants, were always being hired and leaving soon thereafter: Serving my parents was not easy. My mother was nailed to the bed and my father wandered through his overgrown dreams in the sparsely furnished spaces of that enormous house. I was forbidden to touch his things. The little seeds of the fig trees near the gazebo and the myrtle-like guava trees on the mountain that had to be called by their Latin names at home (respectively), *ficus* and *myrcia*, were the royalty above all others. Also deserving the same respect was the *tussacia pulchella*, the honey grass with its red chalice and yellow corollas, which stayed in a fixed position after they were dried. The aroma of the sacred myrrh tree was sad and moist. My father told me how the son of King Kyniras had metamorphosed into a sacred myrrh tree that could never be touched and whose perfume was born from his tears.

Another reason that the young women of golden skin and thick silky hair came and went every hour was because I tried to get rid of them as soon as I heard them repeating my father's stories. In reality, the women who replaced them told the same stories, but used different words and intonations.

I had some favorite stories and listened to them *ad exhaustium*. Did I ever tell you how crazy I was for stories about dolphins, Alexis? I loved the story of a particular type of dolphin they called *souffleur*[5] that came to shore because of an earthquake. Many died, but the ones that survived couldn't resist the lure of *Montanha Pelada*, and since then, they live inside the volcano. When their dreams are populated by sea monsters, they spit out fire. I imagined them like giant frogs dressed in gray with black and yellow smudges. They seemed to me a little bit like the image of Papa Legba,[6] the god of the voodoo pantheon, who points out the way at crossroads to show travelers the right direction.

I never got attached to any of those sweet and docile women with chocolate skin who had to earn a living satisfying my whims. They were both tender and melancholy, and they didn't interest me at all. I wanted to be left alone with my father, his books, and the stories we composed together; and in his absence, I wanted to become the mistress of my own self and share my dreams of flying with my birds. I was very young and assumed that childhood would be the permanent condition of my life.

Until the age we live for our friends, about ten years old, my life was a tapestry woven out of moss and fronds, climbing plants, liana, orchids and vanilla, sugar cane, and the murmuring lament of the bamboo. I had learned to read, write, and multiply, and also learned about the sunset, the taste of cassis and pineapple; and I had already learned how to draw a map of the islands. When Marguerite died, that was what we called my mother at home, my father sent me to his parents' home in France. I left in July. The ship "Peru" took fifteen days to take us across the ocean. My father kept me company on that melancholy crossing as we mourned my mother, and now

---

[5]Bottle-nosed dolphin.
[6]God of the crossroads who reveals the way to the spirit world.

9

it's clear to me that we mourned my childhood and our intimacy as well. We nestled together. My father was my *schutzgeist*, my guardian angel. We shared a restlessness that grew as our distance from the island increased. A sea without end was about to come between us. I already knew France through postcards and the wondrous jelly glasses—green, orange, violet—that arrived like clockwork. Apricot and perfumed orange. I used to stick my fingers in and lick off all the colors of the Caribbean. Salty prosciutto and pâté of duck, fat and greasy. Glazed chestnuts that I ate every night before I went to bed. When I was that age, France was a word that we could eat, and it was very tasty.

After I arrived in France, my life changed completely. The northeast of France was a vast plain, immense surfaces that revealed the earth's roundness and made me want to embrace it. A land of sugar and open sky, where, at sunset, a flock of birds drew moving circles in the air. I had no friends and I was jealous of the birds—their camaraderie and the pleasure they shared. Growing in me was the will to follow them, to get drunk on wind and friendship. I missed Prima Luce and Thesaurus very much. In the spring there was the lemon green of the fields that refreshed my gaze and celebrated the conquest of invincible winter, and everything became a little more joyous, more luminous. Nature tried to keep me company.

My paternal grandparents lived in one of those old family mansions and had very strict habits. In their house I found books that didn't speak about life the same way the books in my Caribbean home did. The books in my grandparents' library introduced me to a new kind of life. The first time I met them, I asked myself if I had enough courage to have an intimate relationship with them. But at that time, I had already begun to feel the need for literature; it kept me from dying of my new reality. At first I only touched those books. A few weeks later I returned to them and leafed through them slowly, so I wouldn't disturb the characters upon whom I had just begun to bestow existence. I had a premonition that perhaps I would discover some friends. But it was more serious than that; I fell in love. With Montaigne. Nothing less. First of all, his name fascinated me. It was a name that warmed me, filling some of my emptiness. And then, I understood that we shared a love for Latin, and I became less lonely. His bilingual writing kept me company. The Latin that he thought "full and thick of a natural and constant vigor" had the gift of being able to signify more than it actually said: "When I see these brave shapes explaining themselves so lively, so profound, I don't just say, 'well said,' I say, 'well thought.'" It was as though my father's spirit inhabited that house with me.

Montaigne was the first of a series of like authors that followed. The Romantics also had their place in my community of friends. The words of Hugo had the power to conjure up and replace the beating wings of my unruly birds because he loved freedom and extolled nature: "Yes, I am a dreamer. I am the comrade / of the golden flowers on the deteriorating wall, / and the voice of the trees and of the wind." The adventurous spirit of his characters fed my need and my desire to know everything. I dreamed a dramatic life for myself filled with innumerable deeds and a tragic death, and listened to myself intone in front of the mirror: "Now I am in chains, my body bound by iron, my spirit imprisoned in an idea. Terrible bloodshed, ruthless plan. I have nothing except a thought, a conviction, a certainty: condemned to death!"

I was hoping that life would present me with a challenge. In Sainte-Pierre life was just there, it was always happening. Keeping your senses alert was all you had to do. When I arrived in France, I didn't know what had to be done to attract life to myself. I couldn't conceive of it. At that age, I didn't know yet that it was my responsibility to build my life myself, and so I acquired nothing. Even later on, I wanted to nourish your love for me, the love I believed was all mine. But in the end, Alexis, all I had left was my love for you.

We never discussed my mother's death, probably because your mother's death took precedence in our conversations. Her passing was an emptiness you were always trying to fill with words. You weren't with her when she died, and you only found out about it a month later, and that had greatly disturbed you. They denied you the right to your suffering, you said; I will never forget those very words. Then listen to me, old friend. I . . . I . . . was alone in my mother's room the day she died and I saw Death approach her and take her away. She was on her chaise lounge, dressed in white as usual, with her eyes open, her hands in an agitated dialogue with one another. Death arrived calm and sure of itself. It made its entrance into the room—coming from no one knows where—crossed the room, brushing lightly against my hair with its long blue pleated velour dress. It was impudent with bluish-rose skin. It looked at me directly. It was such a profound look, like the texture of the moon, of the same color, gray pearl. Its glance was calm and determined. I couldn't do anything. I was paralyzed. I didn't scream or cry. But felt its attraction.

It slammed me up against the door. I waited more than an hour after its departure before I went down to call the maid. And that distressed me very much, much more than the revelation that death existed. It had lived among us since I had been born, but the reality of its power disturbed me deeply. We carry the death of our relatives with us through our entire lives, but that's not the question; the question is life. Our life. It isn't that a life goes away and disappears; it's that life—our life—remains and suddenly becomes heavy and impossible to bear. In looking at the body of my dead mother, I could only think about my father. I was so afraid of losing him that the very possibility replaced the loss I had actually suffered. I didn't cry or touch my mother's dead body, I knew she wasn't there. She would never enter the underworld. I had seen her leaving, flying away. What remained was her body that had always caused me anguish. In the graveyard, I looked only at the scattered flowers in the fields and counted them off by rote in a lowered voice, so as not to frighten away their colors. I was nine years old and I knew that soon I would have to abandon my island. I was going to be orphaned twice.

Leaving for the first time wasn't difficult; the goodbyes weren't painful for me because at that time I thought all departures had returns. My father had always came back. Like the rain. He had confided to me one day that it's only from death you couldn't return. But later, I found out that return is what's difficult, even sometimes impossible, and that childhood, as well as death, is also a place you can't go back to. It isn't time that cannot go back, it is we who cannot go back in time. I never returned to my childhood island. It wasn't because of fear that I never did, no, I even think it was a decision that displayed a certain courage, the courage to exist under the enormity of my sacrosanct childhood. Your childhood was not very happy, Alexis. You cannot therefore understand my decision. But I know that you would have understood it because of the clarity of your thought.

I left my birds there, the parakeets and Thesaurus, the fisherman-pelican, my sailor without a boat. They stayed with my father and, after his departure, were inherited by the new residents. And not too long ago, in the home that had belonged

13

to our family, there was a generation of parakeets that still spoke a few words of Latin. Daniel had been there and had heard them saying "*deo gratias*" in his grandfather's accent, the same French accent that Erasmus ridiculed so much in his treatise *De Rectapronuntiatione*, a dialogue between a bear and a lion on pronunciation.[7] In childhood I read it with my father and knew it almost by heart. And Daniel was able, as I had told him several times, to imagine his grandfather seated at the big dining room table, looking at the image of Saint Michael, saying a prayer of thanksgiving in Latin, blessing the bread and the wine, before beginning the meal. You know, Alexis, this is what keeps me alive—the power of words. Words live forever, they point out the right direction, and express feelings, simply, without removing what complexity exists in them. The words you were never able to find to explain your suffering—the absence of those words prevented us from growing together. You put a real obstacle between what you felt and the words you spoke, an impossible match between the words and the reality.

In France, time began to weigh heavily upon me. The gray days that never ended because they were already painted with the color of the infinite. Weeks of endless tedium went by in a house where every day was the same and only time dared to go forward, but without touching anything. I looked for an exit, and, on a fall day it appeared. My grandparents had decided, without consulting my father, that I would go to a religious boarding school run by nuns and would come back only during the summer vacation. To console my despair, my grandmother used to say that the convent in Argenteuil, near Paris, had also been a haven for Héloïse, her passionate loving despair, and her deception. My grandmother explained that

[7] *De recta Latini Graecique sermonis pronuntiatione dialogus* (1528).

the love story of Héloïse and Abelard was an example of dig-
nity, inner strength, and reparation for human error. Those
were my grandmother's words; the only part I retained was the
one about Héloïse's submission and obedience to love that
proved unworthy. I would have preferred to imagine her as a
rebel and a fugitive, galloping on her courage and determina-
tion, imposing her ideas on the world. With her abandoned
baby Astrolábio—what a funny name—and her solitary but
exemplary love. On the other hand, like me, she let herself be
locked up and imprisoned. I was afraid of having to stay there
for the rest of my life and being castrated as Abelard had been.
To me, being castrated meant being forced to renounce life. To
remain imprisoned, without the possibility of experiencing life
and taking advantage of everything it promised. This thought
alone was a real punishment in itself.

Here, my old friend, I must make one more explanation—
why I spent my nights in bed with other girls: Their company
protected me from isolation. I wasn't narrow-minded about
acting that way. My father taught me Voltaire had said that
prejudice was an opinion without judgment, and there were
good reasons for me to behave as I did. I didn't want to be castrated, I wanted to grow and continue looking for the Firebird
from the Russian tale that my father used to read to me at
night before I had my obscure dreams: "Around midnight,
Ivan Tsarevitch perceived an enormous light that came near the
garden, and soon, everything became as light and clear as if it
were day." It was true, the sacred Firebird did exist, my father
reassured me, and through his words I was able to see him eat
the golden apples, round as the sun, in the Garden of Reality.
If I could find and capture the Firebird, I would have access to
the self-knowledge and happiness that my father had promised
me. I used to fall asleep cradled by this promise.

I never really knew my paternal grandparents. They didn't love me because they didn't love themselves. Hence, their home was hell. To me they were like devils, those web-footed migratory birds of raven plumage, nocturnal habits, and day-blindness that flew over our home at sunset in the Caribbean and announced the coming of darkness and night. Their house was shadowy and in it they lived only for night and its terrors. At night, they were more tolerant of themselves. They cried over the son they had lost and counted the time that passed while they awaited his return from the war. They only went out to go to mass and to the funerals of relatives. They were so attracted to funerary ceremonies and death rituals that they even went to funerals of people they didn't even know. Their home smelled of basil, *ocimum basilicum*, the death plant that wouldn't grow spontaneously on their son's grave since it contained no casket. They burned incense to soothe their son's spirit, which wandered around the house. Their son's soul had become transformed into an unwanted intruder.

It was an anguished atmosphere. The house was a portrait of perenniality and immobility, embraced by ivy, the plant of immortality that had been shaped into hedges. In their home we recited the *Credo* and the *Pater Noster* every morning before beginning one more day of waiting. Prayer was a puzzle and religion put a brake on their desire for vengeance. I think that was why my grandparents steered my father toward real life and its mysteries; he had always lived happily, gravitating around the sun and its light. He was my hummingbird of brilliant plumage.

The time I spent at boarding school was my period of religious revelation. To drown my loneliness and exile, I submitted to the destiny prepared for me by the nuns, those single beings who lived by faith and the love of God and neighbor. I read and reread the lives of saints like Saint Francis of Assisi, my favorite, introduced to me by Dante in the Eleventh Canto of the *Divine Comedy*. His stigmata, his voice, his gestures, his marriage to his beloved wife were the image of love itself. It was love for a woman that made Francis break away from his father. She was an ugly woman whom no one wanted; they all avoided her like death, and yet Francis had united himself to her. I could imagine him in the center of the village square, refusing his father's inheritance, preferring instead the love and companionship of that woman. The chosen woman. It was a beautiful love story, but *in fine* I understood it because they made it clear to me that the woman was figurative poverty. What a deception. I was perfectly indifferent. What I wanted was life and above all love. Because of that metaphor, the beautiful and horrible women didn't really exist. After this hoax I never wanted any more stories explained to me. I wanted to make my own interpretations. To reason by myself.

And then there was the Bible. Every day we read a small excerpt together and reflected on it. God was good, but you couldn't contradict or displease him; you always had to be attentive. It was very suffocating. And later when I was alone at nightfall, I preferred diving into my reading of the apocalypse, that frightening revelation of a vengeful God exacting his price. At the violent end of the world, "the sun becomes black and the moons become red, the heavenly bodies fall like live torches, the earth trembles and the sky disappears." It was a description of a most terrible tale—I knew it by heart: the eruption of *Montanha Pelada* in 1902. The pictures drawn by the apocalypse described the hope of future salvation, a tale out of History. But to me that salvation could only be found on my island close to my birds and to the guardian *souffleurs*, far away from my prison.

MONIQUE

In our home in Sainte-Pierre, we spoke about religion as a mystery of nature, as my father believed in nature and miracles. The shuddering of *Montanha Pelada* was a miracle, revealing signs and wonders of its power like the flowers that grew and the birds that returned every year. He believed in the sanctity of the land and the seasons. He respected the dead and the forefathers. Despised money. And I remember that, hanging on the wall in our dining room, in front of the big window, there was an image of the Archangel Michael conquering the dragon, whose mouth spewed water that would restore the rains to the land and bring about eternal return to the primordial time. I . . . I . . . believed in my father and in the hidden treasures that nourished his imagination. He didn't acknowledge the notion of sin, attesting only to the existence of good and evil. It was enough just to look around. Serpents existed and they bit their own tails. "Think for yourself and I'm sure you will discover goodness," he used to say. My father thought I was protected from evil because of my ingenuity, and, because I was a naturally free being, goodness would always be transparent to me. The results of his research and his discoveries showed that the world and its truth existed all over, and it was enough just to look for it. This was his religion, a quest for the meaning of his life, and it was the orientation of mine. Today, I understand that it was his power that motivated me to find the meaning of my life.

I'm going to tell you something about my love for you, Alexis. At the time we met, I was, like all well-educated young ladies of my age and experience, lacking all expectations regarding marriage. I didn't expect anything special from marriage except that there would definitely be an exchange: I would be transferred from depending on my grandparents to depending on my husband. Otherwise, I would live the same life. Maybe I would have children. I didn't know. It was a question that I didn't ask because others would decide for me, as usual.

Concerning my body: I only knew about its childhood. Its freedom. The pleasure of feeling the touch of my father's lips on my baby cheeks, and the unending kisses all over my hair that made me so happy. His hands on mine, the sugary smell of his tobacco, the arms that picked me up, and, above all, the gaze that pacified me. The pleasure of caressing the feathers of my talkative birds and pelican's pouch, that membranous pouch under his beak where he hid his fish. I was the only one who shared his secret. Feeling his closeness on my neck. My birds were so sweet and their contact gave me so much pleasure. Yes, I knew my body well when I was a child. It wasn't forbidden to me. I could explore it and show it off. The fine long legs that weren't united because of the "*montanha pelada.*"[8] The short silky hair that adorned the entrance, so good to touch. The hair that got goose bumps and laughed. Small pleasures that would make you catch your breath while exploring the sacred fire hidden in the tunnel that existed there inside. That's where life was: discovering the immense possibilities of the body.

Let me tell you about my first time. My first sexual pleasure. Like every other thing that I didn't share with my father, I found it by myself. It was completely unexpected; I didn't know there was a physical pleasure that could come all by itself from inside my body. I was flying, suspended in the air. I had already learned the pleasures of watching the sea, of finding birds in their nests, eating salty grains of sand, passing

---

[8]This plays again with the notion of the bare or naked mountain, the hairless childhood anatomy of the *mons veneris.*

my hand over my skin, and caressing the beard and the wrinkles on the corner of my father's lips as soon as he fell asleep on his chaise lounge in the late afternoon. Those pleasures existed by themselves—they were things, or representations of things, I was able to describe—but that day the pleasure happened all by itself. It came about without any intervention and it existed inside me only. What power! It was an experience that took me over.

There was a tree in my garden, more friendly than the others, who allowed me to ride her, galloping. It was a chestnut tree, *sloanea*, whose thick branches, cascading down to the ground, made it easy to climb, and where my father had hung two ropes that made up a swing. When it rained hard, I liked listening to it as I sat on the branches surrounded by the leaves. The rain's conversation became clear and understandable, more organic. By nightfall on that day, I hadn't yet returned home. Suspended on the swing by the legs with my head down, I propelled my body back and forth and saw the garden upside down. The shadows projected a universe into that space. With the movements that I made by swinging my body, I approached the ground and immediately glided away from it again. Then, after that exhilarating and sensuous dance, when I wanted to get up so I could sit over the seat, the effort of pulling my body slowly erect made me feel a sudden enormous pleasure. It began inside the labia, covered by small hair, animating a tunnel that I was able to imagine but didn't yet know very well. My heart was in that spot. I pulsated from pleasure. It invited me to become abandoned, to feel it and be closer to my body. Unexpected wildness invaded first the lower part of my abdomen and then spread throughout my body. It affected my head the most, hanging down as though it weren't attached to the rest of me. For awhile I was able to balance comfort and surprise. Pleasure. I tried once again and still again, but it never happened a second time. It was a revelation and a revolution. Something had looked inside me and understood sensations I didn't know I had and couldn't control. This discovery distracted my attention from my own body and focused it onto the bodies of others. I wanted to talk to my father about my discovery, but I didn't know the Latin words that could describe it *verbo adverbum.* So I kept everything to myself because the words I knew couldn't describe such an amplitude of intensity. It wasn't modesty, no, it was that I didn't want to spoil the importance of this memory with inappropriate description. Describing too much disturbs the described. Later on, when I did learn the Latin words that could describe what happened, my father wasn't available to me.

I was able to understand all this much better when I read *The School of Women,* a work that revealed the secrets of forbidden emotions, said to have been written by a woman in the seventeenth century in Castilian and then translated into Latin. This was probably the only experience I didn't share with my father throughout my entire childhood because immediately afterwards I became an adolescent, and we became separated by all the taboos of the adult world, which kept us from remaining close. In our conversations.

After I moved to France, I had to hide my body. And my emotions as well, but all I could do was disguise them. My grandparents had no bodies. They were only shadows. Undemonstrative and uncommunicative. They never touched me and avoided looking directly into my eyes. Everything took place in an oblique way. It was as if the denizens of that house existed only to contemplate the past, immobile, like the

21

oil portrait hanging over the fireplace in one of the badly lit and shadowy rooms: A young blond man in military uniform looked straight ahead, gazing directly at the painter and the world of the living that wanted to view him. He had no secrets. The secret was that he disappeared. He had stepped out of himself, overflowing the picture frame, filling up the house, leaving no empty spaces that could contain my presence. So I had to pretend, to act as if I weren't there. To hide my repugnance for the food too acidic, sheets too harsh, water too cold, furniture too austere, glances too critical, tea too much perfumed, clothing without age. To hide my pleasure in well ripened fruit, truly profound books, tranquilizing dreams of heavy rains, letters from my father, family portraits, walks along the sea, touching the horses' manes, and the awakening of my senses.

On a calm fall day, I left for boarding school. My grandparents were sitting in the back seat of the car and I sat next to the driver. My grandmother had told me, quite early that day at breakfast, that I needed to earn the right to receive knowledge. The desire to know, *libido sciendi*, had been born along with me, and I didn't have to cultivate it. My grandmother didn't mean knowledge of the world as a way to attain knowledge of oneself, but she meant knowledge of the world as a way to accept suffering. To learn the life of Jesus and the Saints and the History of Humanity filled with wars, debts, and barbarity. The geography of lost feelings and the mathematical calculations that subtracted days until the moment of the Last Judgment. To learn to live in the future where we would have the status of *animarum post mortem*, when we would already have been judged by God and resting in peace.

The Catholic boarding school didn't make me accept suffering for the simple reason that I had not yet truly found it. I had accepted my mother's death well, and leaving my island had become my ritual of initiation. It was the search for the Firebird that was to mark my passage from adolescence to adulthood. Boarding school made me discover the indifference that was able to dampen my passion, my internal agitation. I never forgot my island, but it remained forever in my childhood. I became another person and began to understand how rare precious things were.

We had to get up early at school. Very early. The sun was still asleep when we awakened tired. We met the new day when a light was suddenly switched on and a prayer—resembling a psalm of the suffering—was mechanically recited aloud by the nun who slept near us. We wore dark uniforms that hid all our femininity. Our bodies needed to be protected from the serpent, they admonished us. He copulated with young virgin women, the cause of the fall from paradise. And in the mornings, above all, there was the mass. Half asleep, we used to go to the small, dark, silent chapel where the candles also seemed sleepy as they flickered reflections of the living dead on the images of the saints.

We listened to the chaplain's prayers and responded automatically, charmed by the music, its cadence, the sonority of the words, and the aroma of sugar and cinnamon. Above all the scent. I remember the gentle warmth filling the air that never left the sacred places during the summer. I can also remember the perfume of the grass, "hunting-devil," the *millepertuis*, that exhales a sugary fragrance of incense that still haunts my memory today. The image of the Virgin with her Son devoured us with their eyes. It was imperative that we not deceive her. We all went through the same motions and we all had the same fears—that we wouldn't deserve their love. On our knees, mouths open, eyes closed, we accepted invasion by the pleasures of the senses. The sensation of a body on our mouths. Our salvation. *Hoc est enim corpus meum.*[9]

Mass was brief; erotic religious ecstasy was long. After the service, we had to receive the chaplain's blessing. He approached us and we kissed his hand. Then he asked us about the state of our souls, and with his man's hand touched our hearts in the place where he could feel our small breasts perfectly. That began to want to grow. Later, we laughed nervously about that intimacy, already waiting impatiently for the end of the next mass. He was our only contact with the world of men. He was the one who chose us, but we stood in line to receive his blessing and unchaste caresses, making us accomplices in a pleasure that we ardently desired to know.

The act of confession was another privileged moment when each of us had the man to herself for that brief space of time. We couldn't make him out very well and he couldn't see us clearly either. All these dark, dense environments helped bring us closer to sin and salvation. We were almost there, but still, there we were not. The soft, sibilant whisper, the lasciviousness of shared sinful intimacy. We could make out his body, especially those hands that we knew so well, his breath, and the noise of his breathing that spoke to our hearts and emotions, and we took great pleasure from the act of telling him what he wanted to hear. He was the one who guided our confessions: what we had done, fantasized, or simply invented at that moment—imaginary things. In that chapel there was no anonymity, unlike confession in any other church. Our chaplain, who should have personified chastity, took part in our game as we imagined ourselves as the Marquesa of Merteuil:[10]

---

[9]"For this is my body," words that transform bread to the body of Christ, spoken by the priest in Latin Catholic mass.

[10]Character in *Dangerous Liaisons* (1782), novel by Pierre Choderlos de Laclos.

"The good priest caused me such deep suffering that I came to the conclusion that pleasure, too, ought to be extreme; and with the desire to learn about pleasure, then came the desire to taste it." You know, Alexis, young women are only mysterious to boys their own age; mature men, they understand women very well. On the other hand, women of your age are incomprehensible to men, as you may well testify.

After attending mass and all its ritual sensuality, we had to return to the dormitory to make our beds and organize our clothing. The newborn day found us a bit ecstatic. Each of us took care of her own space, which was also the communal space. It was difficult for a young only child to share the intimacy of her sleeping quarters with others that she didn't know from Adam. It was during those moments that I think I understood my grandparents' reason for always wanting me to put things in their rightful order—so that I would understand that there was no place for me in France. My space remained in Sainte-Pierre. I had to conquer this new space by suffering, as usual. My life, like religion, was founded on sacrifice and suffering. We left the dorm and went to the refectory, always in silence. Breakfast was brief. We ate, silently, standing, frugally, to the sound of religious music.

We had to get to our classes quickly and begin our studies. We learned a little bit of everything that could be useful to a young woman destined for marriage, children, and becoming the owner and manager of a house. We learned to be docile and obedient, suffer in silence, and love God with all our strength. The kingdom of heaven was a future reality, but we had to earn it here on earth. To the nuns, the present time was already the end of time although its terminus was yet to occur. Hypocrisy and contradiction screamed at us from all sides, but we weren't able to discuss it.

25

At noon we ate, and after lunch we were busy with classes until five o'clock. Classics—language and literature—was the discipline that I liked the best. I imagined Diderot's nun[11] singing litanies, rope around her neck, in the middle of the chapel, at night. In my mind, Susanne was a face in chiaroscuro that followed me; and that, along with my grandmother's blessing, was what I had to remind myself about the dangers of loneliness. Her body was always falling into apparent death. Pleasure and pain revealed themselves as inseparable.

After classes, we had a break. Before we said the rosary, we were allowed to stay together for a while, and we talked about our lives. What brought us together was what time would unearth about the mysteries of the body. We liked to solve the riddle of our future by comparing it to the act of peeling an apple, which, we thought, could reveal how close we were to marriage. The wedding was our future, and the apple, we already knew from Paradise in the Bible. It reminded us that we would always face the need to choose. To choose not between freedom and dependency, but between the quality and the level of our spiritual submission. Freedom only existed within us, we had to keep it hidden. The only way we would be able to discover our bodies was through the signals it sent us. At my grandparents' home all body language was censored. Blood, menstruation, pregnancy. Swollen breasts, pimples on the skin, hair. Although maternity was seldom discussed, the suffering of childbirth was inscribed in our memories. Fear spread without words. My classmates' mothers never spoke of it, and neither of my grandmothers did either. Engraved on women's nature was the understanding that we mustn't complain. We could tell from the expressions of acceptance on

---

[11] *La Religieuse* (p. 1796).

their faces that it was not a joyous act. The representations of women we were able to see were bodiless—fully dressed, shrouded by veils. They were mothers and sisters. They were the faces of acceptance and renunciation. Thus: Woman.

The nun who slept nearby us was always dressed. Even in the middle of the night, when one of us who wasn't feeling well called to her, she would suddenly appear all dressed up like a wandering ghost. We referred to our bodies as though they didn't belong to us; they weren't part of who we were. We didn't look at them because there wasn't enough privacy. Even the mirrors were so small that we could only see our faces in them; our bodies weren't surfaces that could be reflected. And my body had grown and changed so much that I couldn't recognize my childhood body in the shape I perceived under my clothing. I was living in a body that wasn't mine.

The bodies of others—men—existed in images. In art etchings and religious books. The images in the chapel: Christ was always naked on the cross. And there was, above all, Saint Sebastian, his body so beautiful, naked, ripped up by arrows, his clothing spread out on the floor, and his expression so lost, with his sex covered only by a loincloth, a very fine white cloth, that hid everything we wanted so much to see. What was there underneath the cloth that we weren't able to see? Each of us had our own ideas and fantasized individually about the hidden parts in those images of masculine bodies. This forbidden act caused us some fear, and I think it was more than anything else the fear of disillusion. But fear was only a guide that served to accentuate our refusal to submit. What they kept hidden from us actually awakened our desire.

I'm going to try to describe to you, Alexis, what existed in the imaginary of my fifteen-year-old mind, under the veil that covered Saint Sebastian. During the night I dreamed of his body. On my bed, I saw an image step out of Van Dyck's painting. It was the young Roman officer, Saint Sebastian, tied to a tree. His body was full of holes made by arrows, and he suffered. The suffering of a man touches a young woman's own fragility. It throws the world out of balance. I approached him and suffered along with his injured modesty. I liberated him from his martyrdom, removing the arrows and caressing his wounds. I raised the cloth that hid his difference and discovered another arrow—much bigger and more pointed. I woke up frightened.

After dinner we still had to go to the chapel for a little while to say our last prayers before we went to bed. During the day, we had been together but were very isolated in our own tasks and thoughts. A complicit glance, a partly hidden smile, a clandestine message written on a scrap of paper was our way of staying in touch, of not losing our sense of reality, of weaving the bonds of friendship. Getting back to the dormitory at the end of the day, we took off very few clothes because we needed to keep the rest of them on underneath our nightgowns.

I can confess now, Alexis, that it was because of this former promiscuity that our mutual nighttime loneliness was unbearable to me. This was the reason I asked you to turn out the lights; I was afraid you would see my desire. But you were a sensitive man, my dear friend, and therefore truly good, and always gave in to my whims.

But, as I was saying, the nun watched over us, and as soon as we got into bed, she turned off the light and began to prepare her own body for the night. Her bed was separated from ours by a paneled screen that gave her a little privacy. We heard the cold water run. She made her ablutions, purifying herself so she could give her body to the god of her dreams. We imagined that she allowed her hands to touch her neck, taking pleasure in it. We would have liked to have seen her hair scattered over her shoulders and the color of the skin between her breasts, in that very place that no look had yet touched. And we tried to make our eyes become used to the dark, so that we could make out her shadows and contours. We guessed more than we could really see. We exchanged silent and suggestive glances that betrayed our desire. That desire that had to be invented, constructed, because we couldn't attribute a real shape to it.

Later, during the night, when the great majority of girls slept, there were always a few who sought each other out. Who explored the nooks and crannies of bodies they could only see with their hands, their mouths, and their breathing. Identical bodies but not the same. Bodies that could have pleasure without a man's intercession. Petal-like skin appeared from between the sheets and aroused the workings of desire. A moan or a nightmare. The fear and the loneliness. The absence of the maternal kiss. Of a true caress. A complicity that we never spoke about the next day because pleasure had no place in our discourse. When dawn arrived, our bodies became transformed once more into objects of morality.

However, at school there were rumors that contained the truths that we needed to believe in. The rumors spoke about the nocturnal love between a nun and a student. Because of the magnitude of the scandal, this rumor allowed them the privilege of distance and respect. They didn't sleep in my dormitory, but I knew them well; they were both names and faces to me. The young woman was pointed out while people talked about the most daring details of the lost paradise of her body, but I never heard a single word from her own mouth. It was better that way because it conferred more mystery to my desire, which was based on absence. She was the only one of us who had something real between her legs, because she had dared to challenge her body's absent identity by transgressing. When I mentioned this rumor during confession, the chaplain, who assuredly knew about it first hand, referred me to the teaching of Father Morel, the priest in *The Nun*: "What is it about the caresses of another woman that could represent danger to another woman?" I thought about it and decided that if there were something forbidden about it, it was not because the body of one woman desired the body of another woman, but because one of those women was the wife of Christ. Was this adultery, I asked myself from within my internal chaos. The chaplain then instructed me that a young woman must reserve her love, first, for God and, next, for her husband. He didn't talk to me about bodies. The nun took the place of God in his absence. The ninth commandment had not been transgressed.

During summer vacations, I returned to my grandparents' home to spend three months relaxing. Sometimes my father was there also, and we were able to come together only on the realities of the past because everything in our present kept us apart. We took very long walks. We observed nature, acknowledged its changes, its beauty, and listened to the industrious movement of the bees. We focused our attention on the beehives. We could only see them from afar and that distance invested their communal existence with another meaning. They were a real family and we envied them. When I felt that my father was nearby and available, I asked him to tell me a story as if I were still a child. He very much liked to tell stories, wondrous tales, because the words of those timeless stories gave him comfort and security, he who had so much need of internal tranquility from *perpetuum mobili*, erratic and without rest. Simultaneously, because time's transformations on me hurt him, this return to my childhood helped him continue on his way. He didn't recognize me in my adolescent body, and he couldn't bear to touch me or approach my face with his beard to kiss me. He pretended to caress me then turned away immediately. My new body had become an obstacle that placed itself between our affections, and I felt his nostalgia for our former spontaneity. It hurt both of us to think that those moments of plenitude would never return.

We didn't discuss our island. We didn't dare touch on that matter. What happened in Sainte-Pierre didn't interest me. He didn't know anything and he didn't want to know anything about me, the young woman that I had become. He hardly asked any questions about my life, my desires, my dreams. He wanted to retain the image of me as the child that I no longer was.

"The Ice Prince and the Shining Princess" was the title of the story that my father told me during the many walks that we took through the woods on our estate, the last time we met before our wedding, Alexis. We were next to the brook when he began: "In the kingdom of Scythia, in the most icy climate of all, there was once upon a time a prince with a temperament as insensitive as the snows of his country." This eighteenth-century fairy tale has always haunted me, and if I speak about it, Alexis, it is because I will never be able to forget it. I think stories play an important role in the life of every child: at night before she goes to sleep, or at mealtime to encourage her to eat, a special story that will help her construct her identity and make her choices throughout life. "The Ice Prince and the Shining Princess" was my story. I knew it very well, but it always had the power to reveal something different. When I was very small and listened to him tell the story, I was only able to grasp that the poor princess was unhappy and that the prince had rejected her. I was astonished that her father was never mentioned. What was so important to that father that he never came to the assistance of the young "shining princess"? Fathers were always absent from the stories of my childhood. The mothers watched over and helped their sons. In our home, by contrast, it was I who had to protect my mother, enclosed in pain. Nevertheless, my life was also a fairy tale and I felt like a princess. I was convinced by the wondrous tales that I led an exceptional life. So I had to be attentive and on the lookout for the arrival of my prince.

At a later age, it was the prince's love for another that made me really sad, my eyes filling with tears when he said: "How can I be in love with someone who is, in everything, the opposite of all that I find enchanting?" But if the Shining Princess was the most beautiful, how come the prince didn't want to marry her? And I looked again at the image in the book where the Shining Princess, seated near a fountain in a park, saw the reflection of her face on the water's surface.

At that earlier age, my interest was fixed on their adventures, on the descent to the caves, the wild horseback rides through the woods and brooks, and hunting the bear. And also at the surprise of their encounter with a huge serpent whose fantastic scales seemed covered with diamonds, and a black cat with horns and pink wings.

And for a few days I remained agape at the description of white taffeta dresses, decorated with garlands of flowers that matched her coiffure, and I could really imagine myself in that outfit, crossing the park to reunite with my father in his hut. It was he, my prince. He would never abandon me.

And at every age, each time I listened to him tell this tale, I learned more of life's mystery as he imparted more knowledge about life and humanity. Years later, it was my turn to tell the story to Daniel, but it wasn't the same, so much had I added of my own imagination and euphoria. It needed a happy ending. The princess deserved to find her enchanted prince, about that I was sure.

The first time I spent my vacation in Wand, with Princess Catherine de Mainau, who was a friend of my maternal grandmother, as you know very well, Alexis, it was because my father couldn't come to visit me. That was the first summer I spent without him. I wasn't sad. I was disappointed, which was worse: Behavior we don't expect disappoints us and impoverishes our love. It becomes more fragile. My father couldn't have come. His adventures kept him in the islands, I was told then. Later I learned that there was also another happiness. Life, at times, is too long and devouring, my friend, to be nourished with one single love. After finding his other happiness, he spaced out his trips to Europe, and I saw very little of him.

But we continued to write each other once a month, as usual. I never felt replaced. Time, with all the discoveries it contains—joy and suffering—that we had shared, belonged to us and no one else. All the paths we traveled and the mementos we collected still endured. At his death I found all my forgotten letters in a cardboard box. I received them along with the books that we used to go through, page by page, the two of us in Sainte-Pierre, on whose pages I could still see the marks I suppose were left by my enthusiasm. They contained pages we had haunted for so long that *they* could read *us*. And when I looked at the images and phrases from which I had learned to read, everything connected to them at that time came back to me. The warm leather armchair, the faded green lamp that drew a circle of light over the pages, the glass case on the side table, the cushions on the floor where I knelt so as to feel my father's legs close against my breast. Those letters had the smell of my childhood, and a few water stains, as well. One day I decided to read them. I was then able to discover what I had written in those letters: I had created a life that didn't exist. That wasn't mine. And after that reading, I began to love my father more lucidly, more serenely, as I had done before our separation. He knew that the life I represented in my letters was false, but accepted my charade of survival. My pretense. It was useful to him as well.

I discovered that life in a state of need was much more enjoyable than life in the north of France at my paternal grandparents', due to the fact that Princess Catherine was a woman who loved herself. It was this, very simply: She loved herself. She wanted to have her home filled with voices and comings and goings. The pure existence of others was a matter of indifference to her, but because she needed others for her own survival, she used them.

On the day we met, she invited me to spend my summer vacation at Wand on her estate. I had just arrived at the home of my maternal grandmother, Anna Cornelia, and was happy to find myself close to pictures of my mother and the places that had seen her grow up. Sleeping in her adolescent bed and trying to have the same dreams. My joy overflowed and I floated on air when I entered the room where Anna Cornelia and the Princess had taken lemon tea and eaten small plain muffins with bitter orange preserves. My grandmother's teas were comprised of the same menu throughout her entire life. The absence of change was the most fixed characteristic of her existence, her steadiest trait. I didn't expect the princess to be there, and I was astonished by her élan and her laughter, so open and spontaneous. You probably knew her better than I, so I'm not going to describe her, Alexis. But, believe me, I agreed to accompany her on the train, not because I wanted to leave my grandmother's house again, but out of curiosity about her character. She represented a bit of the calm after the storm of murky feelings I had experienced over the years that had just passed. I found her happy and full of life, as I had once been, and it was the princess who led me to my future.

When we arrived at Wand, I could see that there were guests already ensconced there, and they were prepared to stay a few days or even a few weeks in the princess's private life. This discovery didn't please me very much because I had expected to be her only guest. I became content, though, with being her favorite. At least that year. And besides it was naïve of me to think that something similar to intimacy could possibly exist, and, so my first contact with the world disappointed me truly *Homo homini lupus.*[12] *Lupissimus.*

I came face to face with superficial conversations and hypocritical feelings. The princess was rich, and so most of her guests tried to benefit from the acquaintances they could make there, and, at the same time, be able to take advantage of such a pleasant and inexpensive place to stay. For most of those vague characters, silence constituted the absence of meaning, so all they did was talk. They drowned in their own words. The men tried to show that they had wit, exhibiting their knowledge of the world, and the women their false ingenuousness. The first few days after I arrived, I tried to grasp something that had been eluding me: the art of conversation *in absentia*. Here's how I explained it to myself: When they spoke, they addressed someone who wasn't there because the person who stood before them wasn't listening—he was already rehearsing his own reply. And so on, until all the topics of conversation

---

[12]"Man is a wolf to man." Plautus (d. 184 BCE).

admitted in polite society were exhausted. At night they rested, and, the following day, continued the same discussions with the same fashionable arguments.

During my first stay at Wand, when I wanted to escape the vulgarity of the other guests, I daydreamed about receiving nocturnal visits from a man, *ad lib* (as in the time of gods and mythical princesses of fairy tales), whom I didn't recognize, not even his facial features, the following day at the dinner table. He would know something about my feelings, but he himself was a mystery to me. I would attempt to guess who he was from among the men, attentive to a word heard in passing or a stolen touch when being helped out of a boat. Only the desire of his desire kept me company. I didn't close the door of my room, and, despite the evening chill, I used to leave my window ajar. On the one hand, I wanted to be surprised, but on the other, I wanted to facilitate his daring approach. I was already beginning to understand a woman's role in life.

We all took walks and boat rides on the lake, listened to music, and passed the time playing parlor games. There were a few guests who discussed politics privately among themselves, for you know how boring the princess felt these barbarian matters were. She said that having no opinion brought her serenity. The days were calm and what pleased me most were the animals on her estate. Above all, the dogs. They were trained to be hunters, and I often went out with the princess to walk some of them. It was the only time we had any privacy, and the princess, who never spoke of the past, listened while I recited poems and read texts, something I couldn't do in front of her friends on those nights when the full moon lit the park. I was too timid and lived in fear of calling attention to myself. At those moments, the princess loosened up a little and sometimes seemed to be a bit nostalgic, which was not her usual mood.

From that year forward, when I was sixteen, I returned for every summer vacation, and it was already my third stay at Wand the year you and I met for the first time. I hadn't expected to meet you since the princess had never spoken about you. Maybe she thought I would be resistant, I don't know. She was a woman of the world and she knew very well that there is nothing more vulgar than talking about our feelings and trying to impose our own interpretation of things on others. Thus, she trusted her instinct and allowed the situation to unfold by itself. I wasn't looking for a husband; as I already told you, I knew someone would do it for me. No one would ask my opinion, they would only have liked my approval and my resignation. The appropriateness of the decision that was made for me returned to haunt me later in life. I thought I would recognize him. It would not be my duty to build my future, since he would impose it on me. I already had everything necessary to face the world: I was rich, young, and educated. I couldn't count on a marriage for love. The love between two human beings had to grow by itself—it didn't introduce itself, Mother Superior used to remind us. Sometimes we were able to envision passion, but we had to run away from it. Only God's love remains always in us; we only had to nourish that love with prayer and sacrifice to be worthy of it. And, in the face of this danger, we prayed, and the bell rang like the despair of salvation, like the desire to save our lives at that very moment: "Serene light of my soul, brilliant Morning of the most sweet fires, create the day in me. Love that not only illuminates, but makes divine, come to me in Your potency, come to dissolve sweetly all my being." We flushed at the eroticism of Saint Gertrude's prayer.

Nevertheless, I had the hope that at least my sensuality would awaken when my love arrived. I fully expected that when my sensuality was finally awakened, it would become much more visible. I was sure I felt only curiosity. We can conceal curiosity, but not sensuality—it doesn't hide—it flows out of us. Sometimes I sat back observing the men I met in Wand. I looked at them, trying not to hear them, imagining them from a distance, like scarecrows, still and ridiculous. I found them kind, with expressive hands and tender looks, but with vulgar postures. I pitied them. One of the few sentiments that puts people off and separates them is pity, which lends no meaning to existence. The chaplain who heard our confessions at boarding school was much more truthful in both his passion for Christ and for his transgression. Compared to him—his power of persuasion about forgiveness from temptation and salvation—all other men that I met seemed like puppets of destiny.

One particular summer, there was a painter from Vienna among the guests. He was the only there to work. Everyone knew that he wasn't exactly an artist, but he was, instead, what you might call a fashion accessory. I'm not saying that he was good or bad as an artist because I feel that those terms are inaccurate. Either you are an artist, or you aren't; it's a talent we find within ourselves. He was a painter because he used brushes to earn a living, attending the bohemian rich, satisfying their whims in whatever way they desired. He produced what they needed to feed their vanity, and he was able to leave his signature on the walls of palaces and castles by immortalizing their last fantasies: race horses, hunting dogs, lovers, children, lakes, mountains, even cars and summer flowers. Everything he painted was so organized and looked so real that it seemed to be fake. It was this ability to recreate the real that gave him all his celebrity. He had made a legend of himself. His paintings weren't extravagant; he knew exactly what he wanted out of life, and he was secure in this success.

He was intelligent and a little rebellious, which is what pleased the princess. She had invited him so that he could paint a portrait of her beautiful mansion, but he frightened me with his fixed and impudent stare. He was the first man who dared look at me openly. In my meetings with the chaplain, everything happened in shadowy, sacred places, and he never looked at me. Saint Sebastian always had his eyes humbly lowered, and I could look at him as much as I pleased, and he never knew. But the painter's look pierced me through. I was never alone with him, running away from his contact. What scared me was not only his gaze on me, but it was also the way he looked at certain things, like cherries or clouds. Gloves laying on the table or an abandoned drinking glass. Maybe you're asking yourself why I'm telling you all this, Alexis. But bear with me, my dear love, in the moment when everything we desire finally comes to us, we aren't yet prepared to receive it. We anticipate learning how to master our emotions. But how much time it takes! Reality always goes beyond what we anticipated, and we end up recognizing that we have been preparing ourselves all our lives for things that won't ever happen. We're never ready for life, but I didn't know it then. Today I know that our life is an exercise that leads us to the quintessential. To love. If we get it, we fulfill ourselves. And our example points out the path to freedom.

At noon in Wand, when we had lunch—seated at the enormous dining table, with the windows open over the park, our senses awakened by the aromas and colors of the delicacies and wines, our faces flushed from walks through the woods, all a little tipsy from the proximity of nature—we all spoke in the usual way, except for him; he remained silent. He didn't touch his meal and refused what the servants offered him with a distracted gesture. He was seated next to me and touched my leg with his. I became one enormous leg. All the rest of my body had disappeared. He did it intentionally, and I became paralyzed. I thought all looks were concentrated on us, awaiting my reaction. Then I ate to forget or to remember better—I don't know which—the pleasure of his nearness. It's true even today that I still remember this man, not because of the emotions revealed to me by his paintings, but because the same gaze that he had the courage to imprint upon his canvas, he aimed at me and everything that pleased him. At boarding school, we were all together and we were all accomplices, everything related to our bodies was a sin we all shared. It's easier and more stimulating to transgress in a group. In Wand, in the presence of that stranger, I was alone and felt more responsible and vulnerable, as well. I hadn't yet tested my desire and my fear was visible.

I think Princess Catherine understood it all very well that summer; for that reason, the following year she choose you to keep me company so my feelings would emerge. I was disturbed enough to look to you for understanding because you were lost, Alexis, and maybe the princess believed we would grow together without hurting each other. She was, possibly, more truthful than we thought at the time. The hatred she felt towards vulgarity gave her a revulsion for violent sentiments. When we took walks together and I read her selected passages from her library books, she used to tell me, with a dreamy air, that she found it was only literature that could give us the perception of a totality. A few times she suddenly forgot not to be devoured by the magic romanesque art. And next, and next— demonstrating her literary culture—she quoted Seneca: "When we read too great a number of books, we acquire a terrible confusion of spirit." Those were the times I felt I really knew her.

Naturally, your aristocratic name was a guarantee. In the twenties, after the destruction caused by the war and all the lost lives it cost to conquer a space and make a difference, the aristocrats wanted to go on as they always had, sheltered from productive work so that they could devote all their time to human relationships and even to creativity. The comfort of my money gave you the occasion to do so.

The moment I saw you for the first time, Alexis, I understood immediately that you were my Firebird. I should have told you, but I was afraid that my confidence would overwhelm your sensibility. Because, although I didn't expect anything from marriage, as I told you, I expected a lot from life. And when I saw you standing in front of the living room door, trying to not be noticed, with your golden hair and restless look that wouldn't be still, I didn't think of marriage. Of course not. The only impression made on my spirit was that I had discovered the sensation of happiness. Before we were introduced, your image fluttered among the other guests and occupied the time I spent waiting. I was in a hurry to meet you, talk to you, discover you. There was something mysterious about you that filled my complete absence of secrets. I was the image of transparency itself. A happy young woman with no mysteries. Everyone knew my life and my family history since my grandmother regularly attended these gatherings over the summer. My birth in the Caribbean, my mother's death, my father's research, my family life in France, my stay at boarding school, and even my financial worth were facts that all knew. You knew, involuntarily, how to awaken my curiosity, because it existed in me, of course, but had not yet settled itself upon another human being available to me. The princess only brought us together. You were what I needed, and she told to my grandmother who had already begun to worry a little about my future married life.

I already loved you when the issue of marriage was brought up for the first time. I don't think I can say I knew you, but I had invented an image of you that was immensely pleasing to me. It was a love that existed in me and that I projected onto you, and I'm going to be open with you, Alexis. The prospect of becoming your wife disappointed me a little. I foresaw another destiny for our relationship. With a husband, you have to face the vulgarities of the world. Money, payments, society, day-to-day boredom, children, illnesses, family. Yes, like you, I didn't consider family bonds reason enough for social relationships. It was only one more burden. With you, I only wanted to travel—go all over the world—experience pleasure, talk about our favorite books, meet our friends, and listen to the frogs breathe throughout the night. To travel to Venice (it was only later I understood that you didn't enjoy the sea), to live with our emotions, and to exercise our sensuality *ad libatum.* The fact that I accepted your marriage proposal, so courtly and cold, was the first sign that I had abandoned my dreams. I already had accepted, as I explained, that a husband would be chosen for me. It was only that I didn't expect to find that someone whom I actually loved would be chosen as my husband. It didn't even occur to me to question your motivation for accepting the princess's proposal. I thought it was only that you were slightly lonelier than I. Only that.

I knew you didn't love me, but I also understood that my company pleased you and brought you the peace you were searching for at the time. It turned out that I wasn't able to bring you peace, Alexis, but I think I did bring you to yourself. You left me three years later, even more convinced of what you would never accept—the life that society wanted to impose upon you. Close to me, but without my explicit help, you gathered the strength you needed to face your desires and build your future according to your needs. You understood that your unhappiness was only a sign of an erroneous interpretation of your life. I was not part of your future, and that hurt me deeply. Like Susana, the nun, I can tell you that "I will never be able to portray my pain." But I'm almost sure that I will be able to speak about the joy of having shared my life with you during those three years.

I'm not going to describe our life; you know it as well as I do, Alexis. But I'm going to tell you what our encounter meant to me. I had been hoping for you, without any hope of discovering you, as I told you earlier. I loved walking, and you were the ideal companion. You were a little sad and melancholy in front of other people, but when we were alone in the gardens or further ahead in the woods, I could sense your happiness at not having to keep up a pretense, even though you weren't alone. You were more like your true self. My presence freed you from the looks of others. You had finally met someone who didn't displease you, who could accommodate to your restlessness, and could accept you without asking questions. I listened more than I spoke, and my availability was a way for you to forget about life. Courting a young woman and then marrying her was the way you chose to make yourself accepted by society. Marriage was customary, except that you weren't like other people. And despite the decision you made, you couldn't accept yourself. You knew very well that, according to the New Testament, everything we omit doing out of sincere belief is a sin. But belief was something you still lacked. And you found it far away from here. You couldn't find it in our marriage. You never spoke to me about your anguish or your uncertainty. Maybe if you had been able to confide in me and share your suffering, it would have been more bearable. But you decided, Alexis, that I was too young to help you. I found you very secretive and inexperienced, and that attracted me. I had yet to discover you, my love. And I fully expected you would take on the task of drawing forth my love.

The day after our wedding, we went to sleep late and exhausted. We strolled the streets, visited museums, looked at the paintings, and, when tired of images that might prove treacherous, we sat in a church. The dusky shadows, the smell of lavender, the *rosmarinus*, with its stimulating properties, and the shimmering light of the candles brought us together and reconciled us to our bodies. I lived happily and curiously. Marriage was nothing like what I expected.

After we arrived at the hotel, we went up to our room and went to bed without even looking at each other. You said I was tired and that I should rest. I believed you and fell asleep in reassured comfort. You were there next to me, and I knew that it all could still happen. I waited for it.

You slept badly, and, in the morning when I woke up, you weren't in the room, which gave me the opportunity to put myself together the way I wanted to. I had time and the space all for myself. I dressed carefully, and, as usual, you found me beautiful, and that was all. Your morning smile, a far distance away from the intimacy of the room, gave me some security after the rejection of the night before, and I felt good because, for the first time since my childhood in Sainte-Pierre I could do whatever I wanted. Your simplicity and serenity were soothing. Looking back, though, I can see it was a false tranquility. And what astonished me truly was that you were capable of such deception. I realize now that I knew neither you nor myself. And all these years I've asked myself often what you used to think about when your body was on mine. I've already confided in you, my friend, that women's bodies were something I knew about. It was a natural part of young women's education to look for a way of gratifying their desires and needs. They learned how to discover their own bodies and, at the same time, how to keep them away from the danger that could result in more visible consequences. I derived pleasure from touching a body I knew because it was physically similar to mine, it made no demands, there was no violence, and it joined me in awaiting a future happiness. It was neither a sin nor an end in itself, it was a way. A quest. We knew that later there would also be men's bodies. It wasn't either one or the other, but each thing on its own terms. Or even both at the same time. One didn't exclude the other; the goals were the same. To fill our need of feeling less lonely, we became closer to each other. To give and receive. To share a few times too.

I've already told you that during my childhood I wanted to be a boy. I was brought closer and closer to the kind of life my father led through the disapproval I read both in the gesticulating hands of my mother and grandmother and the way they censored my unsubmissive attitude aloud. It wasn't because I desired women's bodies, but rather it was because of the power men possessed to express their freedom. My desire was free, but its expression was imprisoned. I dreamed of traveling and living my life in freedom, without being perturbed by the advances of men and free from restrictions that women had stored up for me.

I'm going to tell you, Alexis, the story that made me dream for some time. At boarding school, there was a young woman my age who had read at home, in hiding, a book I had never seen and whose existence I couldn't have imagined. That girl told us stories that made us laugh and grow. One of those books made us all fall in love; it was a small volume by the British writer Henry Fielding, written in the last half of the eighteenth century and called *The Female Husband*.[13] It told the true story, although fictionalized, of a woman who chose to live her life disguised as a man and who even went so far as to get married to another woman. The real character that interested us was Mary Hamilton, born in Somerset and who later lived in Scotland. At fourteen years of age, she left home dressed in her brother's clothing, and worked as an itinerant doctor. A few years later, she returned to Somerset, her birthplace, under the name of Doctor George Hamilton, and married Mary Price. It was only after three months of marriage, during which time the couple had an intimate relationship, that Mary Price perceived that her husband was a woman. Hamilton, condemned to be whipped in public in the four cities of Somerset, spent six months in prison.

What we liked about this story was the possibility of attaining freedom through a masquerade. Being disguised as a man was being able to live as a true woman. We imagined ourselves Joan of Arc in combat against all prejudice. And the punishment of the condemned that made us afraid—the whip, the prison, and the fire—was only a further attraction. But all that will to transgress abated with the age, and we were submerged into submission. We became kind young women, ready for marriage, the continuation of the mechanism of reproduction, and the perpetuation of the same culture we had challenged in silence. And it was in this state of spirit that you met me, Alexis. Resigned.

You are thinking, for sure, my friend, that many years have passed and that I'm now representing our years of marriage in

---

[13] *The Female Husband or the Surprising History of Mrs. Mary alias Mr. George Hamilton, who was convicted of having married a young woman of Wells and lived with her as her husband, taken from her own mouth since her confinement* (pamphlet, 1746).

the light of my present experience. And you're right, Alexi
except that I'm more indulgent and understanding of you an
more critical in my attitude. If I had written to you the day
received your goodbye letter, you probably would have read
discourse of hatred. I would have represented myself as
victim and would have asked for reparation of all damages th
you caused me. That letter would have done you more har
still. Today, I am able to evaluate the scope of your courage an
recognize your integrity. We need time to mourn rejectio
Especially if it's rejection of a body that didn't yet have time
know itself and from which so much was expected. And yo
probable acknowledgment returns me to the Ice Prince of m
childhood: "How will I be able to love someone who is, i
everything, the opposite of all that enchants me?" What hu
me in your rejection was the rejection itself. The feeling of lo
doesn't mean anything when you're in pain. It wasn't your lac
of love for me or your desire to leave to meet other people an
have other adventures in which I wasn't included; no, it w
knowing that my body hadn't been able to learn to seduce yo
and that it repelled you. By killing the desire of another, m
body also killed its own desire. You often need an entire lif
time, or another occasion for mourning, like the one I have
this moment, to become reconciled with life.

*****

I was the one who decided we would live in Woroïno, just as
was the one who made almost all the other decisions we face
I thought at the time that you wanted to give me the pleasu
of allowing me to choose what I preferred. And then I force
myself to guess your secret preferences, to give them substanc
make them mine, and then took it upon myself to fulfill the

so that I could please you. Finally it was simple: What pleased me was to make you happy. Life was easy. There were no steps to eliminate, there were no curtains to pull. But you were irremediably closed off in absolute solitude and in absolute indifference to the way our life went on. Giving me the power to make decisions was only a way for you to enjoy more freedom. Choice implies risk, and you had opted for safety. Living with me was only a way to make sure that you didn't have to follow roads that would prove too complicated for you.

Your desires made you guilty. You had not yet discovered that your soul was the castle that St. Teresa of Avila described: "That castle contains in itself several residences: some in the middle, others downstairs, and still others on the side. Finally, in the center, there is the main one, where the most secret things happen between God and the soul." There is communication between the outer and inner worlds so that exchange can occur between the body and the soul. The profane and the religious. And inside, the soul subdivides itself infinitely, and those internal divisions multiply themselves. You had not yet discovered that you could be yourself because you had negated the possibility of being the many, my friend.

I decided that the best thing I could do to please you would be to renovate your family home. I thought that decision would make you happy. Later, according to your confession, I understood that you had only wanted to please your family and remedy, as well, a longstanding lack of money. Your indifference to your home in Woroïno was a mirror of our life, Alexis; we weren't happy because we weren't truthful. The reason I didn't try to seduce you was because I didn't know how. I tried to be as good as they had taught me to be school, to give and take pleasure in giving. But, finally, what I had to give was of no interest to you. And that's why I wasn't truthful. I wasn't being myself, I didn't follow my instincts. I became what my education in that religious boarding school had turned me into.

The manor house at Woroïno pleased me because it was dignified and was the only thing that provided me with a small connection to your inner life. It contained no mystery. It revealed itself immediately. It offered shelter because it had been built with love. The soul of a person who builds a house inhabits it forever. I love homes that not only provide shelter but also have intimate stories: drawers filled with memories and furniture caressed by laughter, where you can hear steps on the stairways and the murmurs of a wood parquet floor stretching itself and revealing its well being. Objects that disappear never to be found again—the house puts a spell on them. Although the gardens at Woroïno had become a mass of overgrown vegetation, long since abandoned, you could still perceive what the layout had been. The garden had fallen into a delirium and overtook the home so as to better express itself. It climbed right over the house, decorating the ancient walls with an abundance of ivy, *hedera*, symbol of happiness, that murmured to the windows on the breath of the wind. The house wasn't sad, only a bit nostalgic. It knew how to deal with the transformations of time and bore the decay pretty well. You could read the state of its soul in the shadows projected by tree branches onto the window panes. It was a *locus amoenus*, and I knew very well that my son had to be born there so that he could truly belong to it. The countryside contained a white mountain very different than the fire mountain of my childhood, except that it was near us in its state of grandiose stupefaction.

Had he grown up at my paternal grandparents' home, my son would have had to assume a state of permanent mourning with no hope of remission. The house smelled of silence and the cold of the cemetery. Should he have stayed there, he would have become just one more shadow, or he would have left, never wanting to return, just like his grandfather. At the home of my maternal grandmother, Anna-Cornelia, life would have also been false. It was a home without joy. Everything that had belonged to my mother was in the same place, not because my grandmother had awaited her return, but because she couldn't deal with so much empty space. She had just continued her life as if my mother were still alive. She had needed those references to my mother's existence so that she could hide all her inner turmoil, to be able to face herself. She continued spending all her time traveling. She felt just as comfortable with friends in Paris or Weimar as she did in a hotel in Japan or Syria. She shared with Princess Catherine the pleasure of easy discoveries, great trips by ocean liner that never ended, as well as the fear of growing old. She had mirrors in her house, but, as you know, Alexis, there were none at the home of the Princess of Mainau. But the grandfather clocks and their pendulums were only ghosts of time, covered with sheets as they were. We could hear them strike the hours but we never saw them. She avoided remaining at her permanently incomplete home, which was inhabited by a permanently happy husband. She brought home souvenirs from her trips all over the world. Huge pieces of luggage stuffed without satisfaction. Objects without any value that only filled up what she perceived as the horror of empty, unoccupied space. Her home was not museum-like, however, because she didn't buy select objects—works of art—she only bought a little peace. Trinkets that eased her wounds.

Nevertheless, the place was very amusing to Daniel who, when he was still very young, was allowed to play with all her things, which were really toys for adults. My grandfather's only interests were his horses and his lands; the home and its contents didn't speak to him, and Anna-Cornelia loved her great-grandchild too much to refuse him an absolutely innocent pleasure that pleased them both: He would handle those objects until they broke and she would have to replace them. Daniel inherited the property, the house, and all it contained. I didn't have the courage to get involved in so much despair. Later on, amid all the confusion, Daniel was able to balance the most contrary tensions, imposing a new energy on the objects he had inherited. He omitted practically nothing, and even so, was able to construct visual harmony. He was able to read the story of his family in all that disarray.

Your family home was my dream come true—the perfect place to live, maybe because I knew that we would never live there. It was too heavy for you and connected you to a past that you tried to deny. The time we did live there didn't serve to unite us but led you alone on the path to yourself. We didn't share the same bed because, you had argued, I needed to devote myself to the baby. I never felt your body against mine during the night. You were able to reconcile this with yourself because you had gone back to your passion—music. You no longer needed my assistance in finding yourself. In time I came to understand that it was my presence that had separated you from yourself and your passions. Music and lost bodies in the silence of the night.

I remember the first night your body sought mine. I didn't know anything about men's bodies, they had only been an abstraction, and with you I didn't learn much either. I was only disappointed, and your behavior just confirmed what I had come to expect from marriage. Resignation. A few weeks had passed since our wedding and we had only touched hands to warm ourselves or to help each other during our long walks. Your hand on my forehead worried about the fever I didn't have. Your eyes looked all around except at mine, looking elsewhere so they didn't have to see a woman deceived by love. I didn't exactly know how I wanted you to arouse my desire. I only had the desire of knowing, experimenting, experiencing life. Maybe the fear of your rejection kept me away from you. I didn't know anything. I arrived at marriage without understanding what awaited me. It wasn't desire for your body, since I hadn't yet received it, concealed under your masquerade. I didn't know the color of your skin or the depth of your umbilicus. I only had the desire to desire. It was curiosity born of a fear of the unknown that had been forbidden to me all my life.

What helped make some sense of this encounter was the body of Sebastian, the martyr. The first time you touched me, I thought of him. It was night, the light was off, the shades were down. We could feel the thick darkness of the room. My eyes were quite open, gazing at the altar where I knew he was tied up. And I saw his image from the chapel become confused with that of the painting of the Pollaiuolo brothers, in *The Martyrdom of Saint Sebastian*. I needed the bottom of the tranquil and sinuous river, of that distant but quiet village. Of the green of the field and of life that I sensed in the immobility of that distant calm. I needed a description to surprise me. Everything would go well; there was nothing to be afraid of. I untied him, stretched out my hand and helped him come down. I cleaned his body with my tongue, and then my hands tried to remove his arrows and caress his wounds. They were holes like women's sexes. Deep and warm. Alive. I took off my nightgown to embrace him against me so that he could feel the warmth of my body. But he didn't take his clothes off. He didn't give himself to me.

You also didn't give yourself to me, my dear love. I was really alone. There was nothing more to expect. Everything had been said. Sebastian belonged inside your kingdom and there was no room for me in your pleasure.

But today I can look at my reflection in the windows of my room, where I usually can only see that blind luminosity of all snowy mornings of winter, and I know in your unquestionable absence I can truly confess that on that first night I . . . I was there. We spent time at the after-dinner gathering at the fireplace, eyes bent over the pages of our books. It was late and I was tired. I told you that I was going to go to sleep and you answered that you would stay a little longer to finish reading an article you had just started. I went upstairs and entered the room. And as I had done every evening since our wedding, I waited without really knowing how, for the arrival of the Firebird with golden feathers the color of your hair, Alexis. But the apples coveted by the Firebird weren't to be found on our bed.

In the deep of the night I was awakened by your nervous and hesitating steps. You came close to the bed and raised the sheets. The caress of the cloth sweeping across my body as you undressed me left me fragile and sensual. You touched my skin and I flinched. You positioned me on my stomach, raised my nightgown, and entered my body as if it weren't mine. Facing this reality confused me, but even so I didn't have a choice; I could only rise up out of my body and observe, remaining outside myself. When we observe in the dark, we see much better. All our senses become alert. We listen to breathing, a breath that we can't identify. We give it a form. We guess about movements and contours that we don't see and that have no meaning whatever, since they're outside our own flesh. Drops of perspiration illuminate the wrinkles of taut skin expressing

53

itself alone in the dark. I waited for words and laughter. A wonderment of shared sensations. A rain of emotions. A spell. The vertigo of conquering. I thought we would violate all the taboos. Commit sins.

I ask your forgiveness, my friend, I was inexperienced, delirious. And what I was able to guess revealed itself as something solitary and grotesque. It did not emanate from your inner being, it was not ineluctable or impossible to describe. I could name it aloud. I recognized it only as an escape from *tedium vitae*. Much later, after you were absent from my life, I understood that you didn't seek to possess the object of your passion, since that object was desire itself, and that desire couldn't be materialized. And that was your pain, Alexis. Your impossible situation.

That night, like others that followed, your desire fluctuated and tormented you. I was only the knot that established a connection between you and the reality of your emotions. From that moment on, our intimacy became a permanent game. You played. I watched. I withdrew.

We had lost ourselves irremediably, my love, and although I cannot thank you for having left me, I will always be grateful for your frankness. By leaving, you left me defenseless in facing love. I became a bit like Percival who didn't know where he was after several years of wandering on his quest for the courtly ideal, and "he had no notion of the day, of the hour, or the season." I was very young and I expected to experience everything—everything except being abandoned. Speaking frankly, I shouldn't have been surprised, since abandonment has been the most constant characteristic of my existence. During the three years of our life together, I loved the desire to make you love me, and it was only after you left me that I really began to love you. Slowly. I had the privilege of being able to construct the image of love however I wished. And this love occupied the rest of my life. As you can see, Alexis, I think I wasn't a coward facing life. It took a lot of courage to nourish a one-sided love. For love to become the anchor of our lives, we must fill it rather than give or receive it. If we only give, we devour the object of our love, and it doesn't nourish the rest of our life, and if we receive without giving, it's a wasteland.

When I learned you were ill, I sensed that only your physical disappearance would constitute the definitive unity between us. It was confirmed yesterday. Last night, Daniel informed me you had died. Today, all the newspapers report that you were able to move the world with the agitation and despair of your music. However, I already knew about your departure. Yesterday afternoon, I sensed your presence at my door. You were standing with your back to me, and, at the moment I leaned out the window to water my *hedera* that was hanging on to the wall and to life, you turned your head and looked at me more profoundly than you had ever done in your life, my love. It wasn't a last glance, Alexis, but an affirmation. It's been a long time since I've believed in God, and I think we agree about that. At the end of all these years of fear and darkness, I acknowledge that everything in life that could affirm God's existence would also contradict it. But, according to the principles my father left with me, I believe in the generosity of the universe that overflows upon us and that sweeps us into its current. It's useless to try to love things and people in totality. It's enough to love only one part of them and to take pleasure in it. In life, we have to take advantage of the days when the sun shines and when the night is nourished by the waters of hope. Today I know that everything I always loved in you, your mystery and restlessness, helped me to walk through my life calmly and without secrets. Age has brought me happiness.

At this moment, my beloved, you are a piece of nostalgia I feel I must remember. I know that memory is all we have, and that all our suffering is easier to bear if we make fairy tales out of it or if we use it to provide stories for our detractors.

Now, I'm in the autumn of my life, and again I feel the need for the kind of introspection that returns me to the source of my deepest hurt. And if I write you on this occasion, my darling, it's because I know you cannot read me anymore. Now I write to myself. Not for the sake of revelation, but to become more credible. In any event, I know very well that it's the gaze we direct onto things that gives them life. I unfurl into two and look back upon myself. At this moment, what I desire most is to live near the snow and observe the rainbow of my memories, the circling of the birds that populated my childhood. *Ad vitam aeternam*[14].

---

[14]For all eternity.

About the Author

Portuguese in nationality, born in Angola, Luísa Coelho holds a PhD in Portuguese Literature from the University of Utrecht, Netherlands, and has taught at European universities. Additionally, she has degrees in German Philology and Theories of Political Science. She has mastered eight European languages and has published a number of academic articles. Her works of fiction include *O canto de amor das baleias* (*The Love Song of the Whales*), 1992; *Cavalgar um Raio de Luz* (*Riding a Beam of Light*) 2000; *Os espaços do desejo—contos eróticos* (*The Spaces of Desire: Erotic Tales* (2004); and has edited *Intimidades—Antologia de contos eróticos femininos portugueses e brasileiros* (*Intimacies: An Anthology of Portuguese and Brazilian Women's Erotic Tales*), 2005. She has taught at the University of Brasilia in Brazil and at the University Agostinho Neto in Luanda, Somalia.

About the Translators

Both translators are recipients of PhDs and Professors of English Literature at Borough of Manhattan Community College/CUNY, where they teach both Western, Post-Colonial, and Multi-Cultural Literature. They are known in their field through publications, national and international conferences and workshops in literature, translation, literary criticism, and pedagogy. Their collective learning includes a wide-ranging, overlapping knowledge of many Western European languages, film theory, theater, philology, art history, women's studies, and gender studies. They are currently at work on translating both Portuguese women authors and African women authors of Portuguese expression.